Monster Boy's Valentine

BY CARL EMERSON
ILLUSTRATED BY LON LEVIN

visit us at www.abdopublishing.com

Published by Magic Wagon, a division of the ABDO Group, 8000 West 78th Street, Edina, Minnesota 55439. Copyright © 2011 by Abdo Consulting Group, Inc. International copyrights reserved in all countries. All rights reserved. No part of this book may be reproduced in any form without written permission from the publisher.

Looking Glass Library™ is a trademark and logo of Magic Wagon.

Printed in the United States of America, North Mankato, Minnesota.
052010
092010

Text by Carl Emerson
Illustrations by Lon Levin
Edited by Nadia Higgins
Interior layout and design by Emily Love
Cover design by Emily Love

Library of Congress Cataloging-in-Publication Data

Emerson, Carl.
  Monster Boy's valentine / by Carl Emerson ; illustrated by Lon Levin.
    p. cm. — (Monster Boy)
  ISBN 978-1-60270-782-5
  [1. Monsters—Fiction. 2. Valentine's Day—Fiction.] I. Levin, Lon, ill. II. Title.
  PZ7.E582Ms 2010
  [E]—dc22
                          2010006999

Marty Onster and his classmates were wound up like yo-yos.

"Children! Children! Please settle down," cried Miss Taken. "I know you are excited because tomorrow is Valentine's Day, but we have to talk about our class party!"

"You may bring in cards and candy," Miss Taken said. "But if you do, you MUST bring them for every student in our class."

"Even the monster?" Bart Ully sneered.

Uh-oh. Marty Onster felt his monster-ness begin to show. The skin on his forearms started to crawl. He looked quickly at his best friend, Sally Weet. Seeing her sweet face always calmed him down.

"Now, Bart," Miss Taken said, "Valentine's Day is a day for telling everyone that you care about them."

"Even freaks?" Bart snorted at his own joke.

This time, Marty calmed down by thinking about the valentines he was going to make that afternoon.

Right after school, Marty and Sally raced out the door. They went to buy candy hearts with messages on them to put in their cards.

At home, Marty got to work. He carefully folded a card for each student. He cut some cards into hearts. One heart started out a little pointy, so Marty made that one into bat. Then he made a robot and a T. rex. For Bart, he left the card a plain rectangle.

Marty made a special card for Sally. He cut it into the shape of her favorite bug.

Then he chose which candy heart to go with each student. It was hard to pick. Some of them said "I Love You" or "Hug Me." *Gross!* Marty thought. He just ate those. He saved the one that said "Best Friends" for Sally's card.

Just when Marty was finishing up, his parents and baby brother came home from the store.

"Hey, Marty," his dad said, "we got you some stuff for your Valentine's Day party tomorrow."

Marty wasn't sure what to think. He knew his parents wanted him to act more like a monster. He hoped that this time, things would be different.

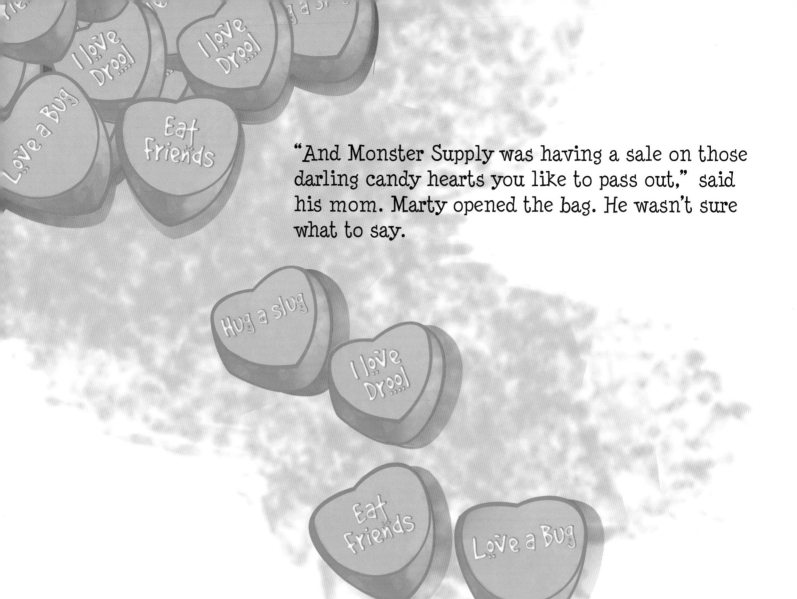

"And Monster Supply was having a sale on those darling candy hearts you like to pass out," said his mom. Marty opened the bag. He wasn't sure what to say.

"Um, thanks," Marty said at last. "I'll be sure to pass those out tomorrow."

When the time for the party came, Marty started digging in his backpack for his cards.

When Marty looked up, he couldn't believe his eyes.

Marty felt his blue monster fur start to pop up. He could feel his fangs growing.

He wasn't sure what to do. His card and candy heart would look like no big deal next to Bart's.

Marty took two big breaths, and his monster-ness went away. He went around the room, passing out his cards. "Here you go, Sally," Marty said. "Sorry it's not, um, bigger."

Sally looked sweetly at Marty. "I'm sure I'll love it," she said. "Here's yours."

"What is that? A bug?" Bart said. "You call that a valentine? I thought you liked Sally!"

Marty could control himself no more. Bright blue fur popped out all over his body. Before he could stop himself, he was flying around the room. He dove into his backpack for his mom's candy hearts. He grabbed chocolates off the desks.

When it was all over, Bart looked like a valentine that would make Marty's parents proud.

When Marty finally sat back in his chair, he and Sally looked at their cards.

Sally leaned over to whisper in Marty's ear. "This is the best Valentine's Day ever," she said.

Contain Your Inner Monster
Tips from Marty Onster

♥ Don't waste time comparing yourself to other people.
It'll just turn you into a monster.

♥ Sometimes the best thing to do is just ignore
people who bug you.

♥ Don't wait for Valentine's Day. Tell your best friends
they're great today!